For Albert and Geneviève

Library of Congress Cataloging in Publication Data
Threadgall, Colin, Proud rooster and the fox/Colin Threadgall.
Summary: A wily fox makes several attempts to steal
the hens from a very vain rooster.
[1. Pride and vanity—Fiction. 2. Roosters—Fiction.
3. Foxes—Fiction.] I. Title.
PZ7.T4115Pr 1992 [E]—dc20 91-15004 CIP AC
ISBN 0-688-11123-8 (trade)—ISBN 0-688-11124-6 (lib.)
First U.S. Edition, 1992
1 3 5 7 9 10 8 6 4 2

Proud
Rooster
➤ and the ◄
FOX

Colin Threadgall

Tambourine Books  New York

There was once a magnificent rooster who was very vain. "Nothing can get the better of me," he boasted. "I'm too clever."

One night an old red fox came to the farm
while all the animals were sleeping.

Rooster knew that Fox
wanted only one thing—
to steal the hens.
"Go away, Fox," he said,
"before I cock-a-doodle-doo
for the farmer to come
with his gun."

"I'll be back," said Fox, and he loped away.

"I'd like to see the fox that can sneak past me!" said Rooster.

The next evening, Fox rolled himself in the ashes of a woodman's fire until he was as gray as night.

Then he crept again to the farm.

Cock-a-doodle-doo!
Cock-a-doodle-doo!
Cock-a-doodle-doo!

Rooster crowed loudly.
Out rushed the farmer with his gun.

"I'll be back," said Fox,
and away he raced up the hill.
"I'd like to see the fox that can
sneak past me!" said Rooster.

In the morning the farmer
went off to market. Fox watched
him go, and then slunk back
into the barnyard.

"I see you," said Rooster.
"Go away, before I set all
the animals after you with my
cock-a-doodle-doo."
"Oh, Rooster," said Fox,
"you have such sharp eyes."
"I have," said Rooster.
"I have the sharpest
eyes in all the world."
"Then let us play a game,"
said Fox. "I'll hide, and
if you can see me, you must
cock-a-doodle-doo as loudly
as you can."
"That's easy," said Rooster,
"I'll spot you every time."

And so he did. The fox hid himself all over the barnyard, but each time the rooster spied him and crowed in triumph.

Cock-a-doodle-doo!

Cock-a-doodle-doo!

Cock-a-doodle-doo!

The game went on, with the fox hiding and the rooster crowing, until the other farm animals grew tired of watching.

"What a fine game," they all cried.

"Can we play, too?"

"Of course," said Rooster, "the more the merrier."

So the farm animals and the fox played
hide-and-seek all afternoon...

and the rooster cock-a-doodle-dooed
all afternoon.

And then, in the distance, Fox saw the
farmer returning.

"I give up," he said to Rooster.
"It must be true. You do have
the sharpest eyes in all the
world."
Rooster swelled his chest
as far as it could go.
"I do, I do!" he crowed,
as the fox ran off.

That night, when the animals lay sleeping
and silent, Fox crept back to the barnyard.
Rooster spied him at once and threw back his
head, but no cock-a-doodle-doo came out.
All the crowing of the afternoon had left
him with nothing but a tiny croak.

"What's the matter, Rooster?" said Fox.
"Has a fox stolen your cock-a-doodle-doo?"
And he laughed as he chased the hens
from the chicken coop.

He chased them out of the barnyard,
up the hill, and into the dark wood,
his mouth watering as he ran.

Now he would have what he had always
wanted...

fresh-laid eggs for breakfast every morning!